A Touch of the Zebras

by Itah Sadu

illustrated by Stephen Taylor

A Touch of the Zebras
Itah Sadu

First published in 2003 by
Women's Press, an imprint of Canadian Scholars' Press Inc.
180 Bloor Street West, Suite 801
Toronto, Ontario
M5S 2V6

www.womenspress.ca

Women's Press gratefully acknowledges financial assistance for our publishing activities from the Ontario Arts Council, the Canada Council for the Arts, the Government of Canada through the Book Publishing Industry Development Program (BPIDP), and the Government of Ontario through the Ontario Book Initiative.

National Library of Canada Cataloguing in Publication

Sadu, Itah, 1961-
    A touch of the zebras / Itah Sadu.
ISBN 0-88961-410-5
I. Title.

PS8587.A242T68 2003   jC813'.54   C2003-900185-7PZ7

Illustrations by Stephen Taylor
Cover and text design by George Kirkpatrick
Models for illustrations: Jeanne-Arlette Parson, Grace Walker, Christopher Malcolm, Rhoma Spencer, and Judith Lezama-Charles

03   04   05   06   07   08   6   5   4   3   2   1

Printed and bound in Canada by AGMV Marquis Imprimeur Inc.

Acknowledgements

I thank the Lester family, in particular Chelsea and Mary Lester for the inspiration.

Dr. Mavis Burke and the Women for PACE for the motivation. Joan Littleford and Ken Setterington for the encouragement.

Michelle Parsons and her family for adding their beauty of spirit to the book.

The two teachers from the York Region Catholic School Board whose names I've forgotten, but who said on hearing the story, "We want to see a book."

Carver Milton Scobie for always encouraging me to push my limits.

To my husband, Miguel SanVicente, and my daughter, Sojouner SanVicente, who listened to the story time and time again with their hearts. Robin Battle who constantly said, "Write the story down."

All God's children,
One love,
Itah.

"I think I'm allergic to school!" Chelsea told her mom.

"Allergic?! I have never heard of anyone being allergic to school," her mom replied.

"But my head hurts, my chest hurts, and some days I can't even move my legs," whined Chelsea.

Every morning it was the same thing over and over and over again. "Shake those Grade 2 blues. It's time for school," said Ms. Rose. Yet Chelsea stayed in bed and would not move.

Most mornings, Ms. Rose was beside herself. She pushed, pulled, dragged, carried, teased, coaxed, bribed with treats, threatened to take away treats, but getting Chelsea to school was like trying to get a camel through the eye of a needle.

"Good morning," Ms. Rose greeted the principal. "How is my Chelsea doing?"

"A delightful child … maybe a little shy at times," replied the principal.

"How is Chelsea doing in class?" Ms. Rose asked the teacher.

"Chelsea is a very good student … maybe a little quiet sometimes…."

Ms. Rose watched Chelsea play with her friends. She even had the air levels in the school tested — everything seemed fine, so why then was it so difficult getting Chelsea off to school?

Ms. Rose took Chelsea to visit their family doctor,
Dr. Sam, who examined Chelsea. She also took her to
see Dr. Lynch, a naturopath, who tested everything and
everywhere. Neither of the doctors could find anything
wrong with Chelsea. Ms. Rose decided it was time to get
help from the family, so she called in Chelsea's aunts and
uncle.

Auntie Asali, Auntie Catherina, and Uncle Juliano came. They listened to the story and then Auntie Asali said, "The girl sounds like she needs a good wash out — maybe she is all clogged up inside. Give her a good teaspoon of cerasee tea, just like our mothers gave us at home in Guyana."

"Give her a teaspoon of cod liver oil," suggested Auntie Catherina.

"I think we should pray for her," added Uncle Juliano.

Poor Chelsea — for the next couple of weeks she received cerasee tea and cod liver oil. Yes, she did get a good cleansing and spent a lot of time in the bathroom, while Ms. Rose prayed hard to get her off to school.

One Monday morning, Ms. Rose entered Chelsea's room only to find Chelsea with a high temperature. Chelsea had worked herself into such a state that she looked green. Ms. Rose sent for a new doctor, who had been recommended by a friend.

"Good morning, Chelsea, I'm Dr. Tara Lorimer, and I'm here to help." Chelsea felt as though she had seen this doctor before. "Let me take a good look at you," said Dr. Lorimer.

The doctor took out her stethoscope and listened to Chelsea's heartbeat. She took her blood pressure and checked her temperature. She couldn't find anything wrong. Maybe Chelsea's temperature was a little high, but . . .

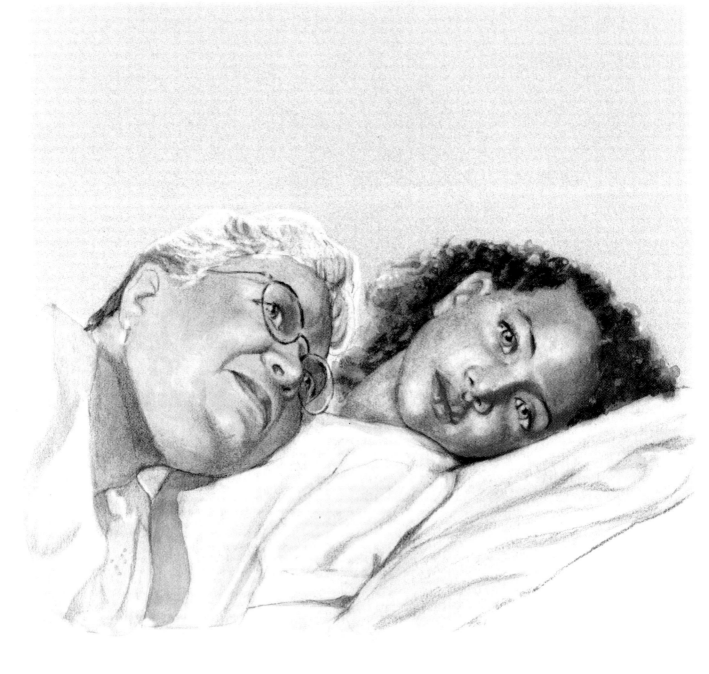

Dr. Lorimer checked Chelsea's eyes, ears, and mouth, and then she checked Chelsea's chest again, this time with her ear. This was the first doctor who had listened to her heartbeat like this. Chelsea found it strange having the doctor lean on her chest. Dr. Lorimer asked Chelsea, "In the morning, does your heart hurt? Do you feel pains in your chest? Do your legs feel frozen? Does it feel like Grade 2 blues?"

"Yes! Yes! Yes!" replied Chelsea enthusiastically.

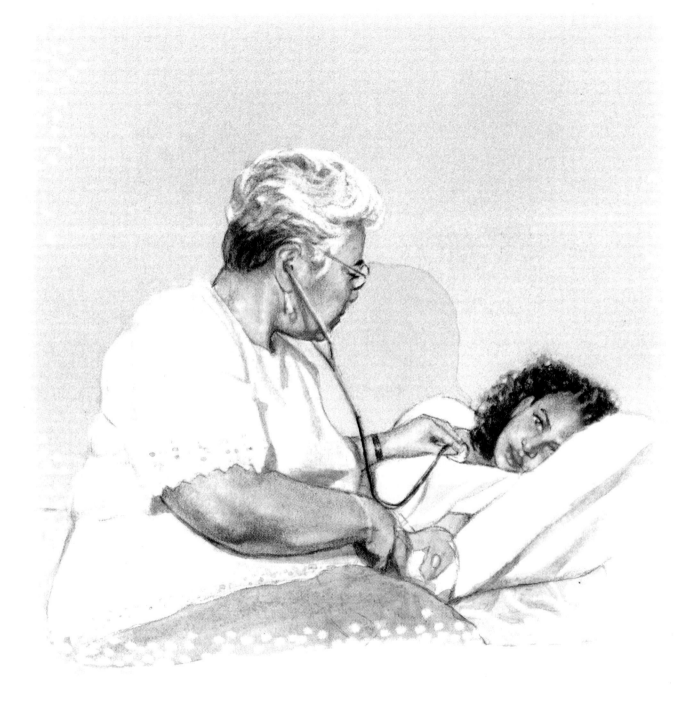

The doctor listened to Chelsea's heart again. "Yes, uh huh uh huh," she muttered. "Tell me, Chelsea, do your head and chest hurt more in history class? Do your legs hurt when you have to choose a group to work with? Do you sometimes feel like a certain animal at the zoo?"

Chelsea opened her eyes wide. She was in shock. This doctor was smart! "How do you know? How do you know about the zebras?" Chelsea whispered.

"I too had a case of the zebras in Grade 2," replied Dr. Lorimer. Chelsea looked at the doctor. Her eyes were a greyish green, her hair was thick and wavy, and her skin was tanned. Chelsea could see herself in the doctor. They had things in common. They shared the same looks.

"Are you telling me that to make me feel better?" asked Chelsea.

"Yes," explained Dr. Lorimer, "When I was a little girl, I was teased, left out of games, and made to feel all mixed up. One day people told me I was black, and another day they told me I was white."

"That's exactly what happens to me!" Chelsea responded excitedly. "Some days I wish I were back in kindergarten."

"Why?" asked Dr. Lorimer.

"Because in kindergarten you can play with everyone," Chelsea explained.

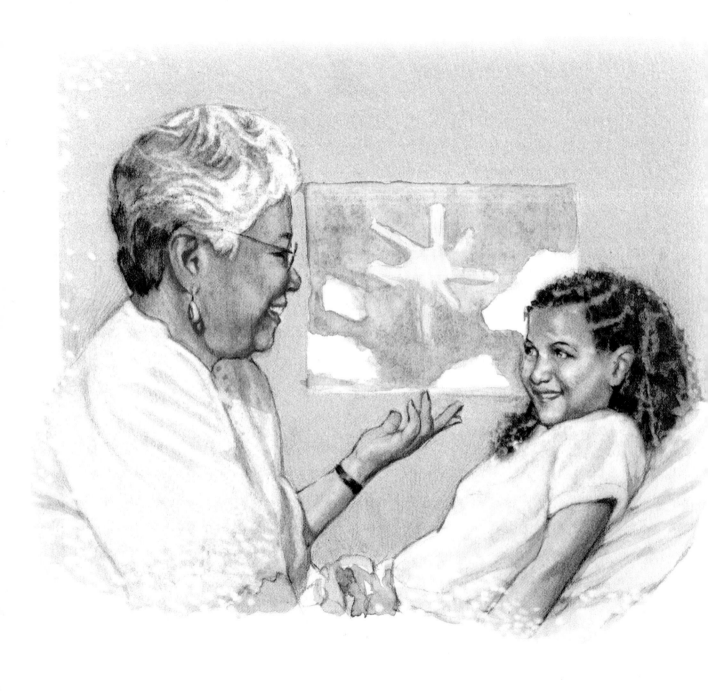

"How did you get rid of the zebras?" asked Chelsea. "I hate having to choose sides."

Dr. Lorimer smiled. "One day at recess, I was standing alone watching the other kids play my favourite games: tag, jump rope, and double dutch. I was pretty miserable. Just then, my teacher, Ms. Sullivan, walked by me and whispered, "Rainbows come in all colours, Tara — always be proud to be of two cultures."

"I thought about what Ms. Sullivan said, and knew that recess would soon be over. I dried my tears and rushed over to play jump rope. From that day on, I chose friends who liked me for being me. Yes, rainbows come in all colours, and I am a mixture, and I am proud to be of two cultures."

"Wow!" exclaimed Chelsea. "Do you still play jump rope?"

"No," said Dr. Lorimer, "I am too cranky and rusty!" Chelsea laughed.

"What's that laughter I hear?" asked Ms. Rose, returning to Chelsea's room.

"Mom, Dr. Lorimer made me better!" shouted Chelsea. Ms. Rose looked at them.

"I believe your daughter had an attack of the zebras," said Dr. Lorimer.

"The zebras?! What on earth is that?" asked Ms. Rose.

"Mom, you know — mixed, biracial like you and dad," Chelsea explained.

"Oh, baby, is that what's been troubling you? How could I not have seen it?"

"It's okay, mom, I'm fine now."

"But how did you chase the zebras away?" asked a puzzled Ms. Rose. Chelsea replied.

"It's like Dr. Lorimer said, mom — rainbows come in all colours, and I am a mixture, and I am proud to be part of two cultures."

And with those words, Chelsea hopped out of bed eagerly and prepared for school.